Disney
BEAUTY AND THE BEAST

Sing-Along Storybook

Based on the story adapted by ELIZABETH RUDNICK

Based on the screenplay by STEPHEN CHBOSKY
and EVAN SPILIOTOPOULOS

Music by ALAN MENKEN, Lyrics by HOWARD ASHMAN and TIM RICE

Disney PRESS
LOS ANGELES • NEW YORK

Copyright © 2017 Disney Enterprises, Inc.
Motion Picture Artwork TM & Copyright © 2017 Disney Enterprises, Inc.

Printed in the United States of America

First Hardcover Edition, September 2017

1 3 5 7 9 10 8 6 4 2

Library of Congress Control Number: 2016948947

ISBN 978-1-368-00423-7

FAC-038091-17202

For more Disney Press fun, visit www.disneybooks.com
For more *Beauty and the Beast* fun, visit www.disney.com/beautyandthebeast

SUSTAINABLE FORESTRY INITIATIVE — Certified Sourcing
www.sfiprogram.org
SFI-00993
Logo Applies to Text Stock Only

Once upon a time, there lived a young prince. He was handsome but heartless. He cared only for outer beauty and material things. The Prince surrounded himself with priceless paintings, extravagant riches, and beautiful objects.

One evening, the Prince threw an elaborate masquerade ball. As the festivities wore on, the Prince surveyed the beautiful subjects before him. He danced with one maiden after another—until, suddenly, there came a knock on the ballroom door. A moment later, a great gust of wind ripped through the open windows, causing the candles to flicker and the ladies to let out startled screams.

Furious at the interruption, the Prince turned to see who had caused this disturbance. In the center of the ballroom stood an old beggar woman. Falling to her knees, the woman begged for shelter from the bitter storm raging outside. In exchange, she offered the Prince a single rose. The Prince was unmoved and waved the old woman away.

"You should not be deceived by appearances," the beggar woman warned, "for beauty is found within."

The Prince threw back his head and laughed cruelly. But as he turned his back on the woman, he heard a collective gasp. He spun around just as the room filled with light!

Where once a horrible hag had stood, there was now a beautiful enchantress. This time it was the Prince who kneeled. He had been put to the test, and he had failed.

"Please," he cried, begging for forgiveness. But his words, the Enchantress knew, were as hollow as his heart. With a flick of her wrist, she cast her spell. The air filled with magic. When it had cleared, the Prince was gone. In his place stood a hideous beast—a beast as terrifying and cruel-looking on the outside as the Prince had been on the inside.

The Enchantress cast a spell on the rose and gave it to the Beast. Then she told him the terms of his curse. The Prince would remain in his beastly form until he learned to love and found someone who could do what he had not—look deeper than appearances and love him for who he was, not what he appeared to be. And if the last petal fell from the rose before that day arrived, he would remain a beast . . . forever.

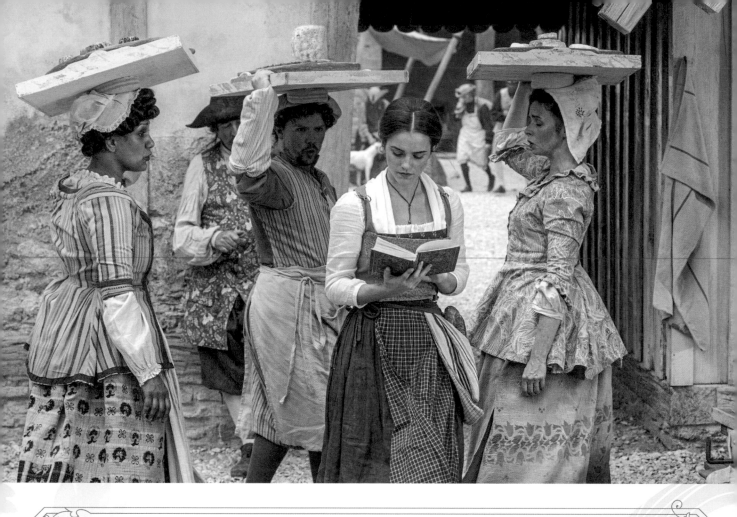

In a nearby village lived a kind, intelligent, independent young woman named Belle. Belle had lived in the same small home in the same small village for almost her entire life. Every day was the same as the day before. She saw the same people and did the same things. The provincial life was fine for the villagers, but Belle yearned for more. She wanted adventure, like she read about in the pages of her favorite books.

While Belle was generous of heart and fair-minded, another resident of the village was quite the opposite. Vain and arrogant, Gaston loved only one thing more than adventure: himself. He knew that the men in the village wanted to be him, and the ladies wanted to marry him.

Belle was the most beautiful girl in the village. That, Gaston reasoned, made her the best. And he, as the handsomest man in the village, deserved the best.

But no matter how hard Gaston tried to win Belle over, she wanted nothing to do with him. Every attempt he made was met with polite yet firm rejection.

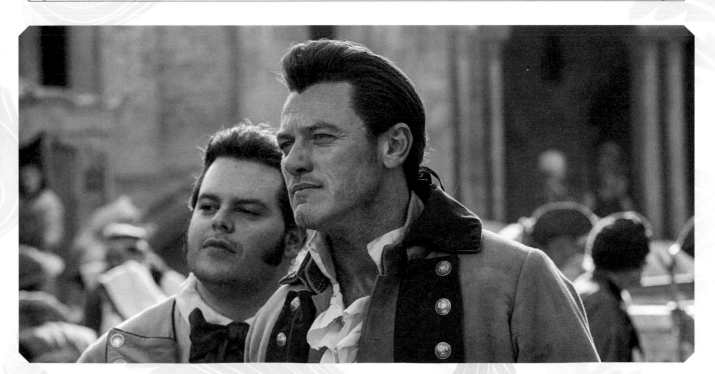

Belle

Music by Alan Menken
Lyrics by Howard Ashman
Published by Wonderland Music Company, Inc. (BMI)/Walt Disney Music Company (ASCAP)

BELLE

Little town, it's a quiet village
Every day like the one before
Little town full of little people
Waking up to say

HOUSEWIVES

Bonjour! Bonjour!

COBBLER

Bonjour!

BUTCHER

Bonjour!

VAGRANT

Bonjour!

BELLE

There goes the baker with his tray
like always
The same old bread
and rolls to sell
Every morning just the same
Since the morning that we came
To this poor provincial town

SCHOOL BOYS

Look there she goes that girl is
strange, no question

NASTY HEADMASTER

Dazed and distracted,
can't you tell?

WASHER WOMEN
Never part of any crowd
'Cause her head's up
on some cloud

LITTLE GIRLS
No denying she's a funny
girl that Belle

FARMER
Bonjour! Good day!
How is your family?

PRETTY FISHMONGER WIFE
Bonjour! Good day!
How is your wife?

CLOTHILDE
I need six eggs
That's too expensive

BELLE
There must be more than this
provincial life

TOM/DICK/STANLEY
Look there she goes the girl is so
peculiar

APOTHECARY
I wonder if she's feeling well

CHEESE SELLERS
With a dreamy far-off look
And her nose stuck in a book
What a puzzle to the rest of us is
Belle

BELLE
Oh, isn't this amazing?
It's my favorite part
because you'll see
Here's where she meets
Prince Charming
But she won't discover that it's
him 'til chapter three

VILLAGE LASSES' MOTHER
Now it's no wonder that her
name means "beauty"
Her looks have got no parallel

VILLAGE LASSES

But behind that fair facade
I'm afraid she's rather odd

VILLAGE LASSES' MOTHER

Very diff'rent from the rest of us

VILLAGE LASSES

She's nothing like the rest of us

VILLAGERS

Yes, different from the rest
of us is Belle

GASTON

Right from the moment
when I met her, saw her
I said she's gorgeous and I fell
Here in town there's only she
Who is beautiful as me
So I'm making plans to woo and
marry Belle

VILLAGE LASSES

Look there he goes,
isn't he dreamy?
Monsieur Gaston, oh he's so cute
Be still my heart,
I'm hardly breathing
He's such a tall, dark,
strong and handsome brute

WASHER WOMEN
Bonjour!

GASTON
Pardon!

BELLE
Good day

HOUSEWIFE 1
Mais oui!

TOM
You call this
bacon?

HOUSEWIFE 2
What lovely
flowers!

CHEESE SELLER 2
Some cheese

WOOD CARRIER
Ten yards!

BREAD BUYER
One pound

GASTON
'Scuse me!
Please let
me through!

CHEESE SELLER 1
I'll get the knife

JAM SELLER
This bread—it's stale!

COBBLER
Those fish—they smell!

BAKER
Madame's mistaken

CLOTHILDE
Well, maybe so

BELLE
There must be more
than this provincial life!

ALL
Good morning!
Oh, good morning!

GASTON
Just watch, I'm going to make Belle my wife!

VILLAGERS
Look there she goes a girl
who's strange but special
A most peculiar mademoiselle
It's a pity and a sin
She doesn't quite fit in

LASSES
But she really is a funny girl

VILLAGE MEN
A beauty but a funny girl

ALL
She really is a funny girl
That Belle!

Belle's father was a music-box maker. One day, he set off on his horse, Philippe, to sell his music boxes. As he entered a dark forest, it began to snow. Then Maurice heard a howl. He and Philippe were surrounded by a pack of hungry wolves!

Just when Maurice was sure they were doomed, he spied a gate. It opened, and Philippe raced through. Seconds later, it slammed shut, stopping the wolves in their tracks.

Looking ahead, Maurice saw a huge castle. Leaving Philippe in the stable, Maurice made his way up the front steps. "Hello?" he called out as the door creaked open. "Anyone home?"

Shivering, Maurice stepped inside. "Forgive me," he said. "I don't mean to intrude. I need shelter from the storm. Hello?"

Suddenly, the smell of something delicious wafted through another set of doors. Following his nose, Maurice found himself in a dining room. "Do you mind . . . ? I'm just going to help myself . . ." he called. Reaching out, Maurice picked up a piece of bread and a hunk of cheese. Then a cup of tea slid into his hand to help wash it all down.

Startled, Maurice looked down. The teacup was alive! Letting out a yelp, Maurice put down the cup—and ran.

Pushing open the castle's front door, Maurice hurried down the steps and fetched Philippe. He paused as he passed a row of rosebushes with glistening white roses. Every time he went on a trip, Belle asked him to bring home a rose. He was sure Belle would love one of these. He reached out and plucked a rose.

"Those are *mine!*"

The words echoed off the castle walls. Instantly, Maurice began to shake. Before him, a giant beast appeared out of the shadows. It walked on its hind legs and wore a long tattered cloak.

"You entered my home," the creature said, dropping to all fours and circling Maurice, "and this is how I am repaid."

Maurice tried to apologize, but before he could get the words out, the creature lifted him off the ground and dragged him into the castle.

Back in the village, Belle was tending the garden when Philippe appeared. Rushing over, Belle saw that the horse's bridle was ripped and he had several scratches along his side. He let out a sad little whicker.

Quickly, Belle put a saddle on Philippe's back and threw on a new bridle. She needed him to take her to her father.

Belle and Philippe raced through the forest. Soon they arrived at the castle. Taking a deep breath, Belle walked through the doors, knowing her father must be inside.

As Belle's eyes adjusted to the dark, she thought she heard whispering.

"But what if she's the one?" a voice said. "The one who will break the spell?"

"Who said that?" Belle asked, turning toward the noise.

No one answered. Instead, Belle heard someone coughing. "Papa!" she cried, running toward the sound.

Belle grabbed a nearby candelabrum and raced up a grand staircase and through the castle. Reaching the very top of a smaller staircase, she realized she was in a prison tower. Through a single door made of iron, Belle heard the coughing again.

"Papa?" Belle called out. "Is that you?"

"Belle?" Maurice's muffled voice answered. "How did you find me?"

Rushing over, Belle dropped to her knees in front of the door. "Oh, Papa," she said, reaching through the openings in the iron. "We need to get you home."

To her surprise, Maurice urged her to leave him behind. "Belle, this castle is alive!" he cried. "You must get away before he finds you!"

"'He'?" Belle repeated.

Suddenly, a roar filled the tower. "Who are *you*?" a voice said. "How did you get in here?"

"I've come for my father," Belle said bravely. "Release him."

"Your father is a thief," the voice replied, sounding closer. "He stole a rose!" the voice roared.

Belle turned to confront her father's captor and let out a gasp. Standing in front of her was a huge creature. It had horns and fangs, and its entire body was covered in golden-brown fur. The word *beast* flashed in her mind as she gazed upon the creature.

Lifting her eyes to meet the Beast's, Belle was surprised to see that his were bright blue and almost human. Then the creature roared again.

"Punish me, not him," Belle said. Her father shouted in protest. Belle was at a loss. She could not leave her father behind. But she knew her father would never allow her to take his place. Forced to make a terrible decision, she agreed to leave, but before she departed, Belle asked the Beast to allow her one last moment with her beloved father.

The Beast didn't move.

"Are you so coldhearted that you won't allow a daughter to kiss her father goodbye? Forever can spare a minute!" Belle cried.

To her surprise, the Beast opened the prison door. Rushing inside, Belle embraced her father.

"I should have been with you," Belle said, hugging her father tightly.

Maurice tried to comfort his daughter, urging her to forget him and live her life. "I love you, Belle. Don't be afraid," he said.

"I'm not afraid," she whispered, her voice barely audible. "And I will escape, I promise."

Suddenly, Belle pushed her father out of the cell and slammed the door shut, locking herself inside. She had made her choice, and there was no going back. Belle's fate now sealed, the Beast dragged Maurice away and threw him out of the castle.

Belle had not been in the cell long when she heard voices. Moments later, the cell filled with light. To her surprise, Belle found herself looking at a small mantel clock and a candelabrum. They were alive! She shouted in surprise. "What are you?"

"I am Lumiere," the candelabrum replied, smiling broadly.

"And you can talk?" Belle asked.

"Of course he can talk," answered the mantel clock, whose name was Cogsworth.

As Belle watched, the two began to argue. It was only a moment before Lumiere took charge, to Cogsworth's dismay, and opened the cell door.

"Ready, miss?" he asked, pointing one of his candles toward the exit.

The odd pair led her back through the castle until they reached a huge set of doors. When the doors opened, Belle found herself looking at a beautiful bedroom.

It seemed she would not be staying in a cell after all.

Back in the village, Gaston was brooding. No one ever said no to Gaston. No one except Belle.

"There are other girls," his friend LeFou pointed out. He nodded over his shoulder. A group of pretty girls sat in the corner, looking at Gaston hopefully.

Gaston barely noticed.

As Gaston's best friend, it was LeFou's job to cheer him up. Running around the tavern, LeFou got the villagers to pay Gaston compliments. No one was as great as Gaston; no one was as strong as Gaston; no one was as admired as Gaston. Gaston sighed. He had heard them all before. And of course, they were all true. He *was* exceptional.

So why, then, did Belle refuse to marry him? If only he had a way to change her mind—some leverage to make her say yes.

Just then, the door to the tavern flew open. Maurice stumbled inside. He was shaking, and his clothing was torn.

"Help!" Maurice cried. "Somebody help me! We have to go . . . not a minute to lose . . ."

"Whoa, whoa, whoa," the tavern keeper said. "Slow down, Maurice."

Maurice shook his head. "He's got Belle . . . locked in a dungeon!"

Gaston sat up straighter, his interest piqued.

"Who's got her?" the tavern keeper asked.

"A beast!" Maurice answered. "A horrible, monstrous beast!"

Instantly, the tavern filled with laughter.

"This isn't a joke! His castle is hidden in the woods." Maurice stopped and looked around the room. "Will no one help me?"

As Gaston listened to the man ramble on, he had an idea. "I'll help you, Maurice," he said, getting to his feet. "Lead us to the Beast."

As they headed out of the tavern, Gaston smiled. He would help Maurice save Belle from the so-called beast. Then she would *have* to marry him.

Inside the Beast's castle, Belle sat in her new room, feeling sad. She was all alone in a strange castle full of enchanted objects, and she was sure she would never see her father or her home again.

Just then, there was a loud knock on her door. A moment later, she heard the Beast demand she join him for dinner.

"You've taken me prisoner and now you're asking me to dine with you?" Belle answered through the door. "Are you mad?"

That was not the right thing to say. She heard the Beast snarl, order his servants not to let her eat, and then storm away.

Luckily, the Beast's servants didn't always listen to their master. Soon a lovely teapot named Mrs. Potts came to comfort Belle. She was the housekeeper of the estate. Before Belle knew what was happening, she found herself sitting at the head of a large dining table. Lumiere led the plates, the cutlery, and the rest of the staff in a grand musical presentation of the most elaborate and delicious meal she had ever had.

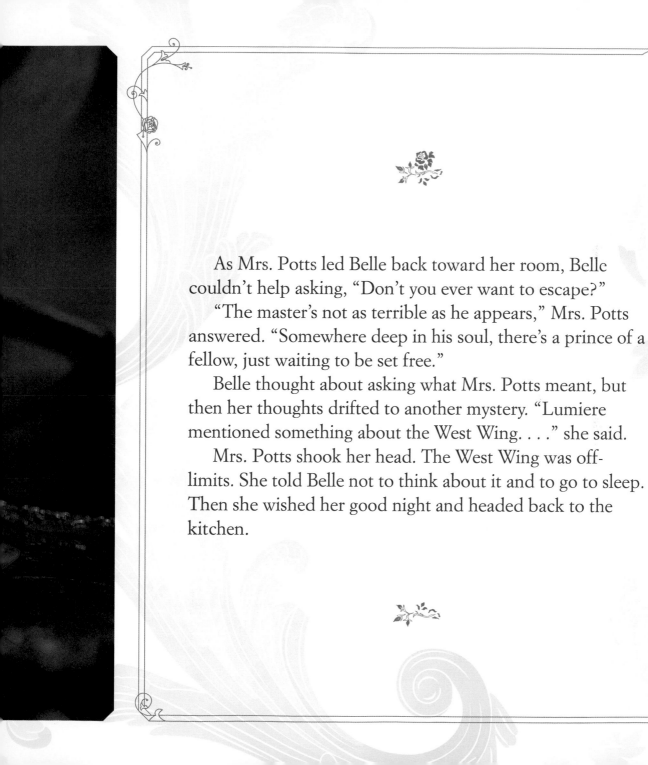

As Mrs. Potts led Belle back toward her room, Belle couldn't help asking, "Don't you ever want to escape?"

"The master's not as terrible as he appears," Mrs. Potts answered. "Somewhere deep in his soul, there's a prince of a fellow, just waiting to be set free."

Belle thought about asking what Mrs. Potts meant, but then her thoughts drifted to another mystery. "Lumiere mentioned something about the West Wing. . . ." she said.

Mrs. Potts shook her head. The West Wing was off-limits. She told Belle not to think about it and to go to sleep. Then she wished her good night and headed back to the kitchen.

Belle waited until Mrs. Potts had disappeared from view. Then she glanced up at the stairs in front of her. If she went left, she would continue back to her room. But if she went right . . . She gazed up the set of stairs as she made up her mind. Taking a deep breath, she started to climb toward the West Wing.

Soon Belle found herself walking down a long dark hallway. At the end of the hallway was a single door. It had been left open.

Her curiosity growing, Belle opened the door wider and walked into a large room. It was clearly the Beast's suite.

Suddenly, Belle's attention was caught by a table. Atop the table was a beautiful glass jar. Inside, a single red rose hung magically in the air.

Mesmerized, Belle reached out and touched the glass.

"What are you doing here?"

The Beast's roar scared Belle. Looking over, she saw him appear out of the shadows.

Terrified, Belle backed away from the table.

"Do you realize what you could have done?" the Beast snarled. One of his arms hit a thin column, causing it to crumble. As its pieces began falling close to the glass jar, panic filled the Beast's eyes. He threw his body over the rose to shield it, screaming, *"Get out!"*

Belle ran out of the castle and to the stable. She mounted Philippe, and the two raced into the woods. Belle and Philippe hadn't gone far when they heard wolves howling. Looking over her shoulder, Belle saw the hungry animals chasing Philippe. A moment later, the horse raced onto a frozen pond.

There was a loud creaking noise as the ice began to crack under the horse's weight. Philippe bucked, keeping the wolves' snapping jaws from closing on his legs. Belle fought off the vicious animals as best she could, but they began to close in around her. Suddenly, as if from nowhere, the Beast appeared.

The Beast jumped into the middle of the wolf pack. Snarling and snapping his powerful teeth, he fought them one by one. He was bigger than the wolves, but the Beast was outnumbered. Then, with a burst of strength, he threw the biggest wolf to the ground. Seeing their leader hurt, the others took off running.

Safe, Belle turned to leave. But when she glanced over her shoulder, she noticed that the Beast had collapsed to the ground, hurt badly from the fight. She paused. He had just saved her life.

Belle helped him onto Philippe's back. Then they began the long, slow walk back to the castle.

Back at the castle, the Beast proved to be a terrible patient.

"That hurts!" he snarled as Belle tried to clean one of his cuts.

"If you held still, it wouldn't hurt as much," Belle said, grabbing his arm and yanking it toward her.

"If *you* hadn't run away," the Beast said, his jaw clenched, "this wouldn't have happened."

"Well, if you hadn't frightened me, I wouldn't have run away!" Belle retorted.

"Well, you shouldn't have been in the West Wing!" the Beast countered angrily.

"Well, you should learn to control your temper," Belle said. And with that, the Beast was still. Belle had made her point.

As the Beast drifted off to sleep, Belle turned to leave. To her surprise, she saw that Lumiere and Mrs. Potts had been watching them the whole time.

"Why do you care so much about him?" Belle asked softly.

In response, Mrs. Potts began to tell her the Beast's story. Once, the Beast had been just a little boy who loved his mother with all his heart. But the boy's mother became gravely ill and passed away. All he was left with was his father. The castle grew dark and cold, and so did the boy's heart. And then . . . the Enchantress cursed him.

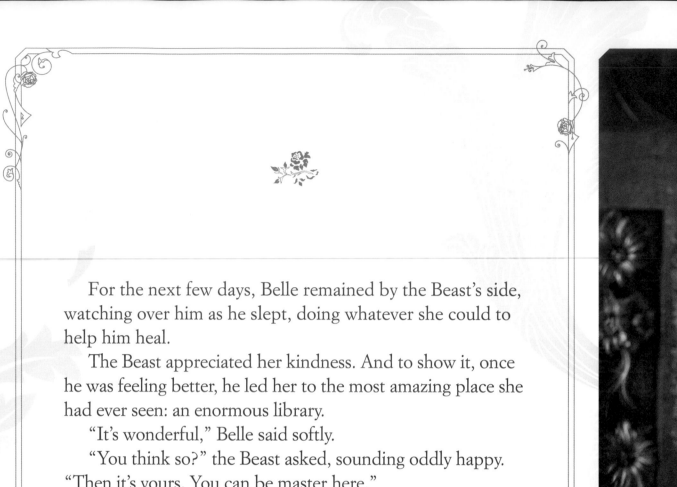

For the next few days, Belle remained by the Beast's side, watching over him as he slept, doing whatever she could to help him heal.

The Beast appreciated her kindness. And to show it, once he was feeling better, he led her to the most amazing place she had ever seen: an enormous library.

"It's wonderful," Belle said softly.

"You think so?" the Beast asked, sounding oddly happy. "Then it's yours. You can be master here."

As the days passed, Belle realized that something had changed between her and the Beast. They were almost becoming friends.

She and the Beast now ate their meals together. When the weather was nice, they walked around the castle grounds together. When the weather wasn't so nice, they had snowball fights.

Belle no longer shuddered if the Beast accidentally touched her with his paw. And she was no longer scared of his fangs when he smiled.

A few evenings later, the staff helped prepare the Beast to share a romantic evening with Belle. The Beast had grown to love Belle. The only problem was that he wasn't sure she loved him in return. He was hoping he would find out that night.

"Do not be discouraged," Lumiere said to the Beast as he got ready. "She is the one."

"She deserves so much more than a beast," the Beast responded.

Mrs. Potts shook her head. "We love you," she said. "So stop being a coward and tell Belle how you feel."

In her room, Belle was getting ready as well. Taking a deep breath, she stepped out of her room and went to meet the Beast.

The Beast was standing at the bottom of the stairs. Both seemed a little nervous. Walking side by side, they entered the magnificent ballroom.

Music filled the air, and beneath the glow of candlelit crystal chandeliers, Belle and the Beast danced together beautifully.

In the corner of the ballroom, the castle staff watched Belle and the Beast dance. Perhaps the curse could be broken after all.

Softly, Mrs. Potts began to sing to herself.

Beauty and the Beast

Music by Alan Menken
Lyrics by Howard Ashman
Published by Wonderland Music Company, Inc. (BMI)
Walt Disney Music Company (ASCAP)

MRS. POTTS

Tale as old as time

True as it can be

Barely even friends

Then somebody bends

Unexpectedly

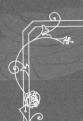

Just a little change

Small to say the least

Both a little scared

Neither one prepared

Beauty and the Beast

Ever just the same

Ever a surprise

Ever as before

Ever just as sure

As the sun will rise

Tale as old as time

Tune as old as song

Bittersweet and strange

Finding you can change

Learning you were wrong

Certain as the sun

Rising in the east

Tale as old as time

Song as old as rhyme

Beauty and the Beast

Tale as old as time

Song as old as rhyme

Beauty and the Beast

As the lights dimmed, they walked out onto the large terrace connected to the ballroom. Belle looked up at the starry sky. The Beast looked at Belle. "It's foolish, I suppose, for a creature like me to hope that one day he might earn your affection," he said.

Belle thought for a second before she spoke. "Can anyone be happy if they aren't free?" she said. The Beast took her back to the West Wing and held up a small mirror. It could show Belle anything she wished to see.

Belle said, "I would like to see my father."

The face of the mirror began to swirl magically. Then Maurice appeared. Belle gasped as she saw her father being dragged through the village square. He looked scared.

"Papa!" she cried. "What are they doing to him?"

The Beast knew what to do. "You must go to him," he said.

Belle didn't know what to say. The Beast had just released her. Softly, she thanked him. Then, before Belle could change her mind, she turned and ran out of the room.

The Beast sighed. The last petal would fall from the rose soon, and when that happened, he would remain a beast—forever.

47

Evermore

Music by Alan Menken
Lyrics by Tim Rice
Published by Wonderland Music Company, Inc. (BMI)

BEAST

I was the one who had it all

I was the master of my fate

I never needed anybody in my life

I learned the truth too late

I'll never shake away the pain

I close my eyes, but she's still there

I let her steal into my melancholy heart

It's more than I can bear

Now I know she'll never leave me
Even as she runs away
She will still torment me, calm me,
hurt me
Move me, come what may
Wasting in my lonely tower
Waiting by an open door
I'll fool myself she'll walk right in
And be with me for evermore

I rage against the trials of love
I curse the fading of the light
Though she's already flown so
Far beyond my reach
She's never out of sight

Now I know she'll never leave me
Even as she fades from view
She will still inspire me
Be a part of everything I do
Wasting in my lonely tower
Waiting by an open door
I'll fool myself she'll walk right in
And as the long, long nights begin
I'll think of all that might have been
Waiting here for evermore

49

When Belle arrived at the village, she found a crowd gathered in the square. It seemed that Maurice had been raving about the Beast, and now Gaston was having him thrown in the local insane asylum!

"Stop!" Belle cried. "My father's not crazy. There *is* a beast!"

Her hand closed around the mirror. The Beast had given it to her so she could see him any time she wished. "You want proof?" she asked loudly. She pulled out the mirror and held it up. *"Show me the Beast!"*

Once again, the mirror face began to swirl magically, until it revealed the Beast. He was slumped against the cold gray stone of the castle.

Seeing the Beast, the villagers gasped in fright. Belle grew worried. She had thought showing the Beast would help save her father. But instead, it had put the Beast in danger.

"Don't be afraid," she said. "He's gentle and kind."

"She is clearly under a spell," Gaston cried. "If I didn't know better, I'd say she even *cared* for this monster."

It didn't take long for Gaston to convince the villagers that they needed to go to the castle and destroy the Beast. Within moments, the once peaceful villagers had become an angry mob. They quickly set off for the castle.

Inside the castle, the staff had gathered together. They were heartbroken Belle had left. Like the Beast, they knew she had been their last chance to break the curse. Now it seemed they would never return to their human forms.

Hearing something outside, the servants peered out the windows. Seeing the light from a dozen torches coming closer, they knew they were in danger. Luckily, Lumiere had a plan. They would act like what they were—household objects. That would give them the element of surprise.

Quickly, the staff got into position. They waited until the villagers had all filed into the foyer. Then Mrs. Potts gave the order. *"Attack!"* she shouted.

The villagers didn't know what hit them. One minute they had been in a room full of an odd assortment of furniture, and the next minute, that furniture was attacking them. The villagers shrieked in fear and began to flee.

While the other villagers ran out of the castle, Gaston proceeded up the stairs. He intended to find the Beast—and kill him.

He ran down one hallway after another until he spotted the Beast, who was standing on a balcony. Pulling out his gun, Gaston approached the Beast. "Were you in love with her?" he asked.

The Beast said nothing. Instead, he turned his back to Gaston.

Gaston fired his gun.

The Beast dropped over the side of the balcony. Gaston prepared to fire again, this time with his crossbow. But when he reached for a bolt, there were none in his quiver. He turned to find Belle behind him. She held up the bolts before snapping them in half.

"When we return to the village, you will marry me," Gaston snarled. "And the Beast's head will hang on our wall!"

"*Never!*" Belle shouted.

Suddenly, Gaston looked outside. The Beast had survived his fall and was climbing slowly back toward Belle.

"Fight me, Beast!" Gaston shouted.

Gaston raised a stone club and approached the Beast.

"Gaston! *No!*" Belle's cry warned the Beast just in time. He turned to see Gaston, who was about to strike him. The Beast reached up and yanked the stone weapon from Gaston's hands. Then he wrapped his paw around Gaston's throat and swung him off the edge of the crumbling footbridge.

"No," Gaston pleaded as his legs dangled over open air. "Please. Don't hurt me, Beast. I'll do anything."

For a long moment, the Beast just stared at Gaston, his features twisted with rage and hate. Then his gaze met Belle's. He wanted to be the man she saw, not the Beast he had become. Slowly, he swung Gaston back over the bridge's wall and set him down. "Go," he said. "Get out." As Gaston scrambled away, the Beast dropped down on all fours and began to run toward the edge of the footbridge. He jumped.

As his front feet landed on the balcony, the Beast smiled. He had made it back to Belle. . . .

Boom! The Beast let out a roar of agony as the sound of gunfire echoed over the castle.

As Belle screamed, Gaston reloaded the rifle. *Boom!* He fired again. The bullet flew through the air and slammed into the Beast. He fell to the ground.

But Gaston's luck, it would seem, had just run out. The stones beneath his feet crumbled. In an instant, there was only empty air beneath him—and a long drop into nothingness.

Belle rushed to the Beast's side.

When the Beast felt her touch, his eyes opened. "You came back," he said.

"Of course I came back," she said, trying not to cry. "I'll never leave you again." Belle choked back a sob. "We're together now," she said. "It's going to be fine. You'll see."

"At least I got to see you one last time," the Beast said. Then his eyes closed. His breathing grew slower. And finally, it stopped.

The Beast was gone.

On a terrace below, unaware of the fate that had just befallen their master, the staff of the castle was celebrating. They had kept the castle safe.

As Lumiere turned to congratulate his old friend Cogsworth, his candles dimmed. The clock was moving oddly. In fact, he was barely moving at all.

One by one, each member of the staff became lifeless, until Lumiere was the only one left.

Soon the terrace was quiet except for the ticking of the clock that had once been Cogsworth. A soft snow began to fall.

The last petal had fallen. The curse was taking effect.

Belle stared down at the Beast. His blue eyes were closed, and she brushed her palm over his cheek. "Please, don't leave me. Come back," she begged.

Belle leaned over and placed a soft kiss on his forehead. And then, ever so gently, she whispered, "I love you."

Instantly, a change began to take place.

Belle watched in disbelief as the Beast's body slowly rose into the air and transformed back into that of a human. He landed softly on his feet, next to Belle.

Belle slowly approached him. In silent disbelief, she ran a finger through the Prince's hair and looked into his blue eyes. *It was him*. Smiling, they leaned toward each other and kissed.

Throughout the castle, the curse gave up its hold. The sun shone, turning the stormy sky a brilliant blue. The cold gray stone walls became a warm gold, and the snow gave way to bright green grass. After so long, everything was coming back to life—including the staff.

Lumiere's candles turned back into arms, while Cogsworth's clock hands transformed into a mustache. Mrs. Potts was no longer a teapot but the castle's housekeeper once more. The castle soon filled with the sounds of laughter.

Belle and the Prince joined the happy crowd and were surrounded by their friends with hugs and cheers.

Belle, the Prince, the castle staff, and all their loved ones from the village celebrated this joyous time with a grand ball.

Dancing across the floor, Belle knew she could never be happier. She was surrounded by her family—old and new. Maurice was there, smiling as he watched his daughter twirl. Lumiere, Cogsworth, and Mrs. Potts were there, as well. All was finally just as it should be.

As Belle lifted her eyes, her gaze met the Prince's. She loved him more with each passing day. And as they danced to the music, they knew that their tale would end as all tales should . . . happily ever after.